THE GREAT FRUITCAKE PICKLEBERRY THEFT

By

Wix and Wrabness
Story Club
At Wix and Wrabness
Primary School

With
Anita Belli

BOOKS

DEDICATION

We would like to dedicate this book to all of our
teachers and parents who help us so much.

Table of Contents

In the Forest by Daniel

1.   The Pickleberrries
and
The Woeful Wizard

When the world-famous Fruitcake Pickleberry bush bears fruit, it is a day of ᴎᴀtᴉoᴎᴀʟ cᴇʟᴇbᴦᴀtᴉoᴎ in the Kingdom of The Noble Princess.

It is the only bush of its kind in the whole of the land and the berries have magical powers.

However, today the wind is whipping the forest floor into swirls of anger as Frank the Wizard creeps into the forest to collect the berries for his latest potion. He wants to make sure he gets there first so he can take all of the berries.

But today, there are acorns and conkers and even Pickleberries skittling around the floor like it is a bowling alley and Frank is worried that all of the Fruitcake Pickleberries on this rare bush will be scattered and spoiled by the wicked wind before he can collect them.

Of course, being a Wizard, he could calm the wind with

Frank the Wizard and Fred the Cat by Daniel

a flick of his wand, but he's lost it, and wonders if his playful cat, Fred, has hidden it. Again.

This is just one of the reasons that Frank is known as *Woeful the Wizard* to all of the creatures in the forest because he is constantly losing, or breaking his wand. The other reason he is known as Woeful is that even when he has his wand, his spells are often clumsy, and badly performed so they backfire. So, instead of calming the wind, it is just as likely that he would create a tornado, or hurricane. A Tsunami is not out of the question with Frank, the *Woeful* Wizard!

2.   The Three Hoot Call

Magic Tree by Robyn-Rose

Meanwhile, Olivia Owl glances down lazily from her perch high up in the tree tops and hoots three times as she lays an unusually large egg.

But this is no ordinary egg. This egg is the most extraordinary egg any owl in the kingdom has ever laid. It is the size of a honeydew melon and is pink with green stripes, red dots, orange stars, yellow lines, small purple dots and some blue squares.

Olivia hasn't laid an egg for a long time and its arrival is as surprising to her as it is to her friend, Sophie.

Sophie flies in to visit Olivia in response to **The Three-Hoot Call.**

This is a call the friends use when they want to see each other. But the Three-Hoot Call also has another purpose. The owls keep a

Magic Egg by Robyn-Rose

look out and warn all the other creatures in the forest if there is danger. Such as a prowling bear who is hungry and looking for lunch. Or even worse, a hunter who is not hungry but looking to shoot creatures for fun. Or The Witch of The Woods looking for frogs and spiders for her potions.

The swirling anger of the wind and **Three-Hoot Call** has made all the creatures a bit anxious this morning.

3. The Golden Fox

The Golden Fox by Robyn-Rose

Hidden in the undergrowth in the darkest part of The Gloomy Forest, the Golden Fox hears the Three-Hoot Call but stays as quiet as he can.

The Golden Fox sees everything that goes on in the forest. He is always watching, and spying on the other creatures like a phantom menace. The Golden Fox is very worried that Frank The Wizard will make another potion to harm his beloved Princess.

Olivia the Owl flies down from her perch when she sees Frank the Wizard approach the Fruitcake Pickleberry bush which is laden with un-picked fruit. She leaves her friend Sophie guarding the precious egg.

All of the creatures in the forest know that the

skin of the Fruitcake Pickleberry contains a magic ingredient which Frank the Wizard uses in his potions. But if Olivia Owl doesn't get there first, Frank will take them all. Olivia thinks that if her abnormally large and colourful egg is ever going to hatch, she will need a store of Fruitcake Pickleberries to feed her chick.

She is certain that this is a magical egg and that her chick will be a very special owl. But only if she feeds it on these rare and precious berries as soon as it hatches.

The Golden Fox by Robyn-Rose

4.   The Meeting

Meeting in the Forest by Daniel

Frank takes a step back, startled, when he sees Olivia swoop down into the clearing and land beside him. He hasn't seen her leave her tree for ages. Everyone knows she is far too lazy to fly anywhere.

Olivia begins to pick berries from the bush.

'Not so fast, Owley,' says Frank, swiping the owl away from the bush. 'I was here first.'

'I need these berries for my chick,' says Olivia, batting her huge wings to keep Frank away from the bush.

'Your what? Since when did you have a chick?' he sneers.

'It's still an egg and when it hatches, these berries will make it even more powerful than you are!' Olivia shouts, over the roar of the wind.

'And I need the berries for a potion,' shouts Frank. What he doesn't add is that he is going to make another attempt to poison The Princess so that he can control the whole of her Kingdom.

.

5. The Thief

Fox by Billy

They begin to fight over the berries on the bush, and the Golden Fox, hidden deeply in the undergrowth, sees his opportunity. Those berries are priceless, but also dangerous in the wrong hands. And he knows that Frank the *Woeful* Wizard definitely possesses **The Wrong Hands.** Frank has already tried to poison The Princess several times and has been defeated only because the creatures in the forest got together and came to her rescue.

The Golden Fox is the leader of the forest

creatures and has become The Princess's closest guardian.

It is, in fact, The Golden Fox who has stolen The Wizard's wand, not the playful (if a little bit evil) kitten Fred. The Golden Fox stole the wand to stop Frank The Wizard from harming the Princess and the forest creatures. The dangerous wand is now hidden in the Palace on the top of The Hill, where The Princess lives. It is locked in a secret vault in the cellar and no-one – not even the Princess, knows it is there.

Now, The Golden Fox has another task which he must complete if he is to save his wonderful Princess. Whilst the wind howls and the Owl and Wizard fight over the berries, Fox does the only thing he can do. He pulls out a sack and fills it with the berries, clearing the bush, which ends up looking more like a prickly hedgehog rather than a magnificent bush of world-famous berries.

Then, the cunning fox slips away into the undergrowth, unseen by The Wizard or The Owl.

No Berries left by Dylan

6. Sharing

When they are both exhausted by their fight, The Owl and The Wizard flop onto the carpet of leaves on the forest floor and agree that they will share the berries.

But when they turn around, they see that the bush is totally NAKED! It looks more like a porcupine than a lush bush of famous Pickleberries!

'How?' 'Who?'

They both speak at once.

Sophie, The Owl's best friend, lands on the ground between them.

'The Golden Fox,' she gasps. 'I tried to warn you but you didn't hear over the noise you were making with that ridiculous fight. And the howling wind isn't helping! I'd better get back up there and make sure that precious egg is safe in the tree tops. Frank, can't you do something to calm the wind?'

'Erm, yes of course. Lots of things I could do, but I erm, I seem to have mislaid my wand!'

'Again?' the Owls chorus together and shake their heads.

'Anyway, where did Foxy go?' asks Frank. 'I need those berries.'

'I need them more,' says Olivia.

'Shall I fly up and see where he is? It looks like he was heading towards the Castle on the Hill,' says Sophie, trying to help. She knows that her friend, Olivia is very lazy and doesn't fly any further than she has to.

'Would you please stay in the tree and guard my precious egg?' Olivia says to Sophie. 'Frank and I will follow the Golden Fox to the Castle on the Hill and see if we can get some of those berries back.'

And so, The Owl and The Wizard set off to follow the fox to The Castle on the Hill.

But they have to cross the Rapid River of Doom first, and Frank doesn't have his wand with him to help. And Owl, of course, is far too lazy to fly over it!

River by Neve

7. Crossing The Rapid River Of Doom

Forest Creatures gather to help, by Mason

Although Frank The Wizard doesn't have his wand, he is good at thinking up solutions to problems and asking for help. So, the problem is, they have to cross the fast-flowing **River of Doom** and neither Owl nor Wizard can swim very well.

Meanwhile, some of the forest creatures have

gathered around to help.

'Who has a good idea?' asks Frank.

Micah the Lobster says: 'Let's build a raft,' and he sets about making an ingenious plan for how to do it.

How to make a raft by Micah

How to Make a Raft, by Micah.
You will need: Reeds, Logs and Bark.
The reeds will hold the logs together.
How to make the Paddle: Find a strong stick and a piece of bark.

Neve the crocodile says, 'use pumpkins as stepping stones. Or better still, I will carry you all across the river on my back!'

Frank and Olivia look at the crocodile's fearsome teeth and huge wide mouth, and are not at all sure about climbing on her back.

Pumpkins by Neve

Meanwhile, Harry the Horse says 'Let's build a bridge!' but the others think that will be too much like hard work, all except Micah, who is already drawing a plan for a bridge and working out where they can gather the timber from.

Harry The Horse sees that the river here is not very wide. 'I reckon I can jump over this river with Frank and Olivia on my back,' he says.

Harry the Horse leaps across the river

'Well, we've never seen you jump over anything,' say the three frogs, Dylan, Adam and Daniel, which makes Olivia and Frank very unsure about this plan.

'Surely we'll fall off his back when he jumps!' says Frank, not wanting to fall into that fast-flowing River of Doom, which looks very angry.

Mason, the spider says that he can spin webs and shoot strong lines across the river. But Frank doesn't really want to do a death slide across this rapid river either. It sounds far too adventurous for him.

Meanwhile, Neve the Crocodile has gathered all of the biggest pumpkins she can find and placed them in the water like stepping stones.

Frank decides to go with the pumpkins, but is alarmed to see that Neve The Crocodile is in the water, swimming alongside him. He must make sure he doesn't fall in!

Crocodile in the water by Neve

Owl on the Raft by Micah

8. The Crocodile
and The Raft

Olivia is more sensible and decides that she will try Micah's raft. It looks so strong and beautifully made.

That is, until Harry the Horse climbs on board with all of the other creatures and it begins to sink.

Olivia flaps her wings and manages to stay out of the water, but the other animals all fall in. Neve the crocodile swims around furiously trying to help everyone out of the water, except Harry. He is a very strong horse and he swims ashore quite easily.

Then, in one, terrifying leap, the creatures all look on in amazement as Harry the Horse leaps across to the other side of the river.

All the splashing about in the water topples Frank from his Pumpkin Path.

Rapid River by Neve

"Help Me! I'm Drowning! I can't Swim!" shouts Frank, but he is washed away towards the terrifying rapids. Suddenly, he feels the crocodile's jaws close around him.

"This is not how I wanted it to end! I only wanted to follow the Golden Fox and get the Fruitcake Pickleberries for my potion!" he wails, woefully.

Neve The Crocodile climbs onto the opposite shore of the river and gently opens her mouth to let Frank out. He climbs out of her mouth and lies on the riverbank looking up at the trees around him. The face of Harry the Horse is staring down at him.

He is grateful to Neve for saving his life, but before he has time to thank her, he remembers The Quest to get The Fruitcake Pickleberries!

The face of Harry the Horse is staring down at him by Mason

He hopes that Olivia Owl is stranded on the other

side of the river, because then he can continue The Quest by himself and get there first.

But, when he sits up, soaking wet and covered in crocodile drool, he sees a raft heading towards the shore, with Micah paddling confidently, and Olivia Owl sitting at the front like a conquering hero. The three frogs, Adam, Daniel and Dylan, are on board and also Mason, the spider.

Frank is gutted. They have all survived the rapid River of Doom. But he has a head start, so, he turns away from the river and wonders if he can catch The Golden Fox before the others arrive. Secretly, he is hoping that the raft sinks!

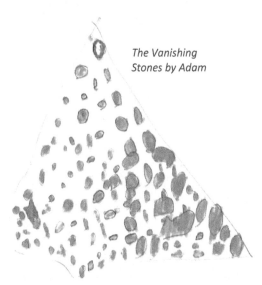

The Vanishing Stones by Adam

And then he sees, in front of him a huge cliff which he will have to climb without any of the creatures to help him, and no wand or spell book.

9. The Vanishing Stones

The Spider groped a Powerful web down the cliff.

By Adam

Frank the Wizard definitely needs help with this problem. They would all have to work together to get over this cliff and into the forest beyond.

So, he decides to wait for them all to come ashore and notices that Olivia the owl is the only dry creature amongst them. And he also realises that if she chooses to fly, she could get to The Golden Fox first and take all the berries. So, he decides to take control.

He sees that there are stones sticking out of the cliff which will provide hand and foot holds, but as soon as he gets hold of one of the stones, he only has 20 seconds before they vanish and he is left hanging with nothing to hold on to!

In no time at all, Mason the Spider climbs the cliff and drops a silk line down for Frank to hold onto. But it is only a thin line which looks like it won't be strong enough to hold Frank for very long. So, Mason has to work extra hard to make more lines which the other creatures plait together to make a much stronger rope.

The Spider's Silk Ropes by Daniel

One by one, they are pulled up to the top of the

cliff. All except for Harry the Horse. Even Mason The Super Spider can't make a rope strong enough to haul Harry The Horse up a cliff!

So, Harry decides to gallop around the cliff to another part of the shoreline where he can scramble, sure-footed to the top.

10 Has It Hatched Yet?

Frank the Wizard is feeling much more confident by the time they get to the top of the cliff. And he realises that when they all work together, they have a better chance of catching The Golden Fox.

Fox by Billy

Olivia the Owl, however, is feeling exhausted and wishes she could still fly. And she is worried about her egg. Has it hatched yet? Will she be able to hear the Three-Hoot Call if Sophie sends for her?

Egg by Robyn-Rose

Frank gets to the top of the cliff first and is dismayed to see that there is another forest ahead. But he is getting impatient to catch the Fox, so he plunges straight in, deciding not to wait for Olivia, who is dawdling behind him and chatting with the other creatures. He decides to run on ahead.

Wizard running ahead by Daniel

11. The Double-Trap

Frank is just thinking about how clever he is to run on ahead when he trips over something. It feels like a cushion, but what on earth is a cushion doing out here in the middle of the forest?

Then he remembers, too late, what it could be!

The ground disappears beneath him and he feels himself falling deeper and deeper into the earth.

Then, he hears the crashing noise of gears and the

The Overhead Trap by Micah

whooshing sound of the leaves rustling in the trees above his head. He looks up, just in time to see a cage come crashing down onto of him as he is stuck in a deep hole.

And to make matters even worse, It is an ingenious double trap - a deep hole which he himself had dug ages ago to capture The Princess, and covered with leaves.

"How ridiculous," he says out loud, to himself, "to fall into my own trap!"

And he is very glad that the others aren't around to see him. But then, he realises that he needs the others to help him get out.

He hears a rustling in the leaves around him.

"Help me out! I'm STUCK" he shouts as loud as he can!

"Should've watched where you're going," says a familiar voice from the undergrowth.

Two amber eyes surrounded by black fur

Fred the Cat by Daniel

peep out of the bushes and pounce on the cage which has descended from the treetops and now covers the hole.

"Fred, my beloved kitty cat! Thank goodness it's you! Have you got my wand?" Asks Frank.

"No! Why would I have your wand?"

Frank is deflated. "Oh. I assumed you'd taken it!"

"Noooo! Why would I do that?" asks Fred.

"Well, if you haven't got it, I can't magic my way out. I'll have to **think** of something!"

The Trap by Harry

"Or **remember** something," says Fred, enjoying seeing Frank stuck in his own trap.

"*Remember* what?" says Frank "That there's a cave at the bottom of the hole you dug. And you can simply climb out! If you're strong enough that is!" says Fred the Kitten.

Frank isn't sure that he can climb out of the hole through the cave but he is not going to admit that to his kitten. So, he decides that he has to give it a go. And he needs to do it quickly before Olivia and the other creatures turn up and laugh at him. Because that would be the worst thing ever; to have all the forest creatures laughing at him.

12. Following the Fox

By Harry

Meanwhile, Olivia The Owl is sitting happily on top of Harry the Horse with Micah the Lobster, the three frogs and the Spider and trotting though the woods looking for signs of the Fox. Neve the Crocodile has decided to stay by the river where she is happiest.

Dylan the frog spots some Fox tracks and Harry plunges into the undergrowth to follow the trail almost knocking them all off his back as

Frogs by Dylan

he ducks under low branches.

Mason the Spider decides to climb a tree so that he can see further ahead and help them to find the Fox.

And there, ahead he sees The Princess's Castle on the Hill, sticking up above the tree tops and almost touching the clouds.

The Castle by Mason

13. The Princess's Castle

Mason the Spider has never been inside the castle and decides that he would love to see what it's like. So, he scootles and swings his way through the treetops, arriving at the castle just ahead of the others.

Owl by Neve

And then they hear the unmistakeable sound of ...

The Three Hoot Call!

They all hear it!

Frank the Wizard stuck in his trap

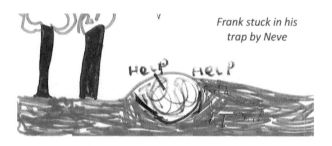

Frank stuck in his trap by Neve

Fred The Cat waiting by the entrance of the cave for his master.

Fred the Cat by Daniel

Harry the Horse with the three frogs and the lobster on his back.

Mason The Spider as he climbs up the steep walls of the Castle.

The Princess who comes out onto the battlements to see what is going on.

And the Golden Fox who is scurrying around in the cellars and dungeons of the castle.

The Golden Fox by Robyn-Rose

But it is Olivia who is the most alarmed. She flaps up and down and forgets that she can't fly and launches herself off Harry's back

Three Hoot Call by Neve

and soars up, higher and higher until she lands with a thump at the feet of The Princess on the Tallest Tower of the Castle.

Princess's Castle by Mason

14. On The Battlements

The Princess by Billy

Mason The Spider climbs over the bricks at the top of the tower and is surprised to see that Olivia The Owl is already there.

The Princess is standing very tall on the tower of her castle and quite surprised by an Owl landing at her feet.

Then, she sees Mason the Spider and screams.

Well, he is very big and very hairy.

This brings the guards running to the tower to protect The Princess. Olivia Owl flies up and settles on the tower ramparts next to Mason the Spider and begins to talk as fast as she can!

She tells the Princess everything that has happened so far. How Frank the Wizard wanted the Fruitcake Pickleberries but she needs them for her chick. And then The Golden Fox stole all the berries and was heading towards her castle. They had no choice but to follow The Fox. So, they have crossed the rapid River of Doom and climbed the Cliff of the Vanishing Stones to get here, with help from some of the Forest Creatures.

*Guard
by Harry*

"And I had to leave my friend Sophie guarding my precious egg, which has surely hatched by now because why else would Sophie send out a **Three Hoot Call?**' Olivia cries, and the Princess bends down to comfort the distressed owl.

Sophie in the tree by Daniel

36

"So, Frank The Wizard is on his way here?" asks The Princess.

"Yes. He's tracking The Golden Fox," says Mason The Spider.

The Golden Fox by Billy

"Well, I haven't seen Foxy, have you seen him, guards?"

"Not today, Your Highness," says the Leader of the Guards.

"And he has all of the Fruitcake Pickleberries?" asks The Princess.

"Yes. Frank wants them for a potion," says Olivia Owl.

"Oh dear. Not another one! That will surely be disastrous!" says the Princess. "Guards, if you see Frank approach the Castle, arrest him and throw him into the Dungeons."

Wizard by Dylan

Guards by Harry

15. The Golden Fox's Confession

The Golden Fox by Robyn-Rose

Then another voice comes out of the shadows.

"May I suggest, your Royal Highness, that you bring The Wizard here and speak to him first?"

"How did you get in without us seeing you?" the Leader of the Guards asks The Golden Fox, who slips out of the shadows into the moonlight which is lighting up the tower. The Fox bows to The Princess.

"Still as cunning as ever, Foxy? Why do I need to speak to Frank? Why not just throw him in the dungeon and chuck away the key?" asks The Princess.

"Because I think he may have learned a lesson, Your Majesty. And it is surely better to have such a powerful force on our side, Your Highness?"

"My Chick will be much more powerful than Frank The *Woeful* Wizard, but only if I can get those Pickleberries," wails Olivia the Owl.

Guard by Daniel

Then, she turns around and sees that Mason The Spider has disappeared. She hopes he has gone to find the Fruitcake Pickleberries.

But this is taking far too long and she needs to get back to her chick with those precious berries.

The Princess speaks. "Foxy, did you steal the Fruitcake Pickleberries?"

He kneels down in front of The Princess and the Guards surround him.

"Yes, your Majesty. BUT, only to stop Frank the Wizard from trying to poison you again!"

The Princess is thinking about Fox's words. Can she trust him? He has always been loyal and faithful to her and now he seems to have committed a crime to help her! What should she do?

But she can't think over the noise of the howling wind and the wailing Owl who is at her feet, tugging at her long gown and crying that her Chick needs those berries.

And over all of the Kerfuffle, they hear it again.

The Three Hoot Call.

Three Hoot Call by Neve

16. Olivia returns

Olivia can wait no longer.

This is urgent.

She spreads her wings which are as wide as three of the crenelations on the castle wall, and hovers in the air above them all.

"I am so sorry your Roy*al Highness Majesty*! But I have to respond to **The Three Hoot Call.**"

"Yes of course. Let us know what your chick is like, when it hatches!"

And Olivia soars up into the air and flies over the treetops in the moonlight, enjoying the feeling on the air whooshing by and the wind in her feathers.

Down below, she sees the Princess on her Tower

and Frank the Wizard approaching the Castle at the same time as Harry the Horse and the other creatures.

Olivia wishes she was taking the Fruitcake Pickleberries back with her, but she trusts The Princess and is excited to see her baby chick hatching.

*****

Olivia lands on the branch of her tree and sees Sophie flapping around busily.

"Oh, my word. I thought you wouldn't make it in time! The egg has cracked, and Little Chick is fighting its way out! Did you get The Fruitcake Pickleberries?"

Egg in the tree by Billy

Olivia is delighted to be here in time to greet her chick, but also sad that she hasn't got the Pickleberries to make her chick stronger and more powerful than any wizard in the land.

When it is fully hatched, she wraps her new-born chick in her huge wings and settles down on the tree for a nice long sleep.

In the dungeon by Mason

17. The Great Escape

Meanwhile, Mason The Spider has found his way into the cellars and dungeons of the castle just in time to see Harry The Horse, The Three Frogs, Dylan, Adam and Daniel, and Micah the Lobster, all thrown into a dungeon together. Frank the Wizard is nowhere to be seen!

Mason creeps into the dungeon through the prison bars and is already hatching a cunning plan. It involves Micah The Lobster, all of The Frogs, and Harry The Horse.

"Ok. So, Micah, can you use your claws to pick the lock on the door?" asks Mason.

Micah clicks away at the lock and it springs open.

"Harry, use your strength to push the door open," whispers Mason.

Micah the Lobster by Dylan

With the door wide open, Dylan, Adam and Daniel the frogs can hop through and wait for Mason to tell them what to do next.

"Shhh. We have to be really quiet! The guards are all on the Tower with the Princess, so, Harry, you stay here and search for those berries. We'll head to the Tower. Let's hope the Princess likes Frogs more than she likes Spiders," says Mason.

In the dungeon by Harry

He leads the frogs through the labyrinth of the castle

corridors and passageways, up and down stairs and in and out and round and round. Until they finally arrive at the tallest tower where they find the Princess with Frank the Wizard in chains in front of her surrounded by guards, and the Golden Fox still on his knees.

There is no sign of Olivia The Owl.

Olivia flying home by Harry

Three frogs by Daniel

18. The Distraction

"Ok," Mason whispers to the frogs. "Hop about and cause a distraction."

Which they do! Dylan lands at the Princess's feet and hops up and down, whilst Daniel, the daring, leaps up onto the Lead Guards shoulder and blows a great big raspberry in his face!

The guard drops his pike and screams and runs from the Battlements, and the other guards follow.

Adam who is a bit younger than the other two frogs, hops onto the back of the Golden Fox and gazes at the Princess in awe!

The Princess picks Adam up in her hands.

'How cute. Where did you come from?' she asks.

'And if I kiss you, will you turn into a handsome Prince?'

But she decides not to try it, because a handsome Prince will complicate the story too much!

Fox is brave now that the guards have gone. "These are the creatures who helped Frank to get here," Fox says to The Princess.

"Oh, I see. You are the Three Adventure Frogs! How wonderful to meet you! But why did you want to help Frank The Woeful Wizard in his attempts to poison me?"

Mason the Spider decides it is time he says something.

"Forgive us, your Highness. We were helping Olivia Owl to get the berries back for her chick which surely will have hatched by now."

The Princess thinks about this. "Yes. She flew home to be with her little baby chick. She should definitely have those berries. Foxy, where are they?" she demands. "Yes. I have decided. Frank, you will stay here in the castle under guard, where we can keep an eye on you. And Fox, I command you to bring me ALL of the Fruitcake Pickleberries."

It is at this moment that Harry the Horse crashes through the doors to the Tower carrying something in his mouth.

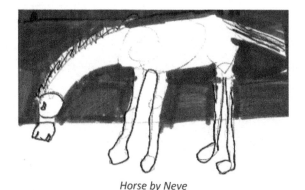

Horse by Neve

19. Princess To The Rescue

"Look what I found in the Dungeons!" shouts Harry, triumphantly.

"Oh, my word. Where did you come from? I haven't seen you in my stables? And what is that in your mouth?" says the Princess.

"My wand," cries Frank the *Woeful* Wizard.

"Mine now," says the Princess and snaps it in two and tosses it off the tower ramparts into the bushes below. "That wand won't be harming anyone else," she says.

Harry bows to The Princess. "Your Highness, I brought these other creatures here on my back, including Olivia the Owl who cannot fly..."

The Princess looks confused.

"So how did she fly away to her chick when she heard **The Three Hoot Call**?" asks the Princess. "I saw her fly with my own eyes. So why are you lying to me?"

Harry is worried that he has upset The Princess, and she might throw him in the dungeons again. But it is Foxy who speaks next.

"It is well known amongst the Forest Creatures, Your Majesty, that Olivia Owl is far too lazy to fly!"

The Princess laughs. "Not anymore," she says.

Then she turns to Harry who is standing proudly beside her.

"Would you let me ride on your back through the forest so that I can see all of the wonderful and kindly forest creatures for myself? And we can visit Olivia and her new baby chick!" She is excited and jumping up and down, clapping her hands.

"Of course, your majesty."

"Ok then. Quick let's go now before the guards come back. They won't let me out on my own and especially not at night!"

"But you won't be alone, your Majesty. The Three Adventure Frogs and Micah The Lobster will be coming with us as your guard," says Harry.

The Princess leads Harry down the steps to the ground floor of the Castle with the Lobster and three Frogs marching closely behind, proud to be *The New Guard*. Then she stops suddenly and they all crash into each other.

"FOXY!" she shouts loudly.

"Yes, Your Majesty?" he says as he sneaks in

beside them.

"Get me those berries! NOW! I'll take them personally as a present to Olivia and her Chick! And tell the guards to lock Frank in the cellar and keep a close eye on him."

Princess on the Horse by Mason

20. The Moonlit Forest

They tiptoe as quietly as they can out of the castle, leaving Frank the wizard, still in chains, stuck alone on top of The Tower, until the guards clatter up the stairs and drag him down to the dungeons.

Mason The Spider decides to take the quick way down the high castle walls and meets them all at the entrance to The Castle.

"I'll navigate from the treetops," says Mason.

And their final adventure begins.

Princess riding in the forest by Billy

The Princess is delighted to be riding freely on a fast white horse through the forest in the moonlight. She has never enjoyed this much freedom and loves the constant chatter of Micah the Lobster, Dylan, Adam and Daniel the frogs and even laughs at their jokes.

She has also noticed that the wind has stopped howling and the full moon is lighting their path. She is gloriously happy to have met her new friends and have her worst enemy locked up in her castle.

Suddenly, Harry the Horse rears up and swerves off the path and The princess has to cling to his mane to stop herself from falling off.

Then she sees it.

A large green crocodile slithers across their path and Harry has swerved to avoid trampling on it.

"I heard you lot coming from a mile off," says Neve The Crocodile. "Thought you might like my help to get over the Rapid River again?"

"Have you seen Olivia?" asks Harry.

"Yep. Flew in like a white ghost crossing the moon a while ago. That precious egg of hers seems to have hatched."

They all cheer at this and then Neve sees The Princess on Harry's back.

"Oh, Your Highness. Pleased to make your acquaintance," says Neve. "But I'd be careful if I was you in this forest at night! You never know who you might bump into!"

They climb down the cliff (which is much easier than climbing up, because Mason's ropes are still there.)

Then they cross the river with Neve's help. Micah is delighted to find that his raft is still safe on the banks of the river and The Princess is happy to sail across with Micah, Dylan, Adam and Daniel Frogs as her guard.

Harry, showing off to the Princess, does his death-defying leap across the river again, to cheers from his friends.

Chick hatches by Robyn-Rose

21. Baby Chick

The friends are close to the Owl Tree by now and they can hear the gentle chirping of a new-born chick.

Sophie is on watch whilst Olivia and the chick sleep, so she hoots a greeting to them which wakes Olivia.

'Looks like we have visitors,' says Sophie.

Olivia shakes her head in disbelief that The Princess has come all this way to see her chick. Holding the baby tightly in her beak, she swoops down into the clearing to greet her friends.

The Princess holds out the sack, bulging with Fruitcake Pickleberries and Olivia begins to feed them to her chick. The chick opens its large golden eyes widely, takes the berries and chirps loudly. It eats the whole sack full of berries and then nuzzles The Princesses hand.

Princess visits Owl by Robyn-Rose

"How adorable! I want to take her to live with me in the Castle!" says the Princess clapping her hands excitedly.

But Olivia is firm. "When she is grown, I will bring her to you, your highness, and if she can be of service to you, then she can live at the castle. But for now, she must live with all of us in the forest and grow and learn to be a wise and kind owl. It is very important if she has powers that she knows how to be kind and use them to help everyone."

In the undergrowth, no-one sees or hears The Golden Fox watching and listening. And Foxy is wondering if he can allow this baby owl to grow up to be so powerful.

The End

Glossary of words

Some words you may not have come across before

Crenelations 	A battlement in castles, in which rectangular gaps occur at intervals to allow for the launch of arrows from within the defences.
Ramparts 	a defensive wall of a castle with a broad top, a walkway and often a stone parapet.
Kerfuffle	a commotion or fuss.
Woeful	Full of woe. Or very bad at doing something.

About the Authors

The members of Wix and Wrabness Primary School's story club, The Story Squad are:
Adam, Billy, Daniel, Dylan, Harry, Mason, Micah, Neve and Robyn-Rose
They range in age from 7 to 11. These children were the main authors and illustrators of this book.

Other children played a role in the programme and helped to devise the original story, but are not final contributors to this book.
Freya, Jacob, Jake, Owen, Thomas B. Thomas T.

The children each brought their unique brand of creative ideas, words and pictures. The story grew rapidly with far more ideas than could be encompassed in one book, and voting was essential to choose from many different options in the plotting.

All of the ideas and story plotting was theirs. Anita Belli simply wrote their words.

About the Programme

I have long wanted to develop a co-authoring programme with children - writing their ideas as a 'ghost' writer might, and sharing with them, the process of writing and publishing a book. And when the children of Wix and Wrabness Primary School came up with such a great idea for a story, through Story Club, I knew that this was a group of creative children I could work with. I extended the club in their school so that we had an extra half term to make this project happen.

In the first session, we divided the group into two and each group devised a character by asking a lot of questions and voting on options. They presented their characters to the bigger group and I challenged them to write a scene where the two characters meet.

We discussed story structure and mapped out a framework for the story of the Wizard and the Owl, but by then a host of secondary characters had also emerged. As often happens with characters, they began to take over, the children deciding on the problems the characters would face. The solutions were harder to find, but by putting forward various ideas, and voting on the merits of each idea, bearing in mind the plot which they had devised, we came up with a strong story outline and some very well devised character traits. This is the process I go through to write novels, and seeing the children embrace it, was inspiring. The children began to draw the pictures for the story, and I brought a children's illustrator, Charlotte Cleveland, into the group to support their drawing.

This book is a result of their ideas, co-authored with Anita Belli. The core group of nine children completed the programme. Their enthusiasm for the project never wavered over the two half terms we worked on the project, although the group did change slightly after the first half term, when some members had other places they needed to be at that time on a Tuesday after school.

The Story Club Programme happened in 7 schools across The Tendring District of Essex during 2022, for an hour after school, funded by Hervey Benham Charitable Trust and Arts Council England.

After school clubs create a sense of belonging, improve social skills, provide academic support and make learning fun and creative.

The focus of Story Club was on developing the children's creativity and creative skills by playing games, drawing and writing challenges which encouraged them to:
- Use their imagination
- Ask questions
- Make connections between ideas
- Solve (story) problems

Creative skills which will support them to move forward with curiosity and creativity wherever their journey takes them.

HERVEY BENHAM CHARITABLE TRUST

Supported using public funding by
ARTS COUNCIL ENGLAND

About Wix and Wrabness

By Headteacher, James Newell

At Wix and Wrabness Primary School, we value and prioritise creativity in all its forms. Writing from the heart and from experiences is central to our vision for writing.

Children don't always have a large 'bank' of memories or an array of synonyms to describe ideas with. So, at our school, we help children to develop these creative skills by giving children opportunities and time to imagine, create and explore.

Our **Curious Journals** are one way in which we offer children time and space to write freely, – to 'journal' in the true sense.

To support this type of writing we provide stimuli; real life experiences that inspire children, a curriculum that is arts rich, broad and ambitious. Children see themselves as writers at this school... they know that their work is valued and has worth. A book like this, working in collaboration with an author, embeds these feelings and enables children to write without barriers, without fear and with a true authenticity.

The Great Fruitcake Pickleberry Theft

Our school values 'pupil voice', pupils' own interests and uses these ideas as staring points for extending learning and discovery.

Making connections across subject develops more robust and detailed writing. Writing for children at this school is a life skill, a creative outlet and a therapeutic process.

Our **Platinum Artsmark award** reflects our aspirations for all here, it says, 'this is a school where learning is steeped in creativity and exploration'.

Love Learning, Stay Curious

James Newell

The Great Fruitcake Pickleberry Theft

The characters

Notes for Teachers

Dear teachers and TA's. Please use this book in your classroom in any way you see fit. This book can be used to generate creative writing ideas, or discussions about some of the issues raised in the book. For example, why was Frank always so mean to everyone? Did he get what he deserved in the end? How did Olivia Owl's laziness and inability to fly contribute to her problems? And what is the backstory of these characters?

The book will work for with Ys 1,2,3, and 4, to be read out loud or for upper KS2 children to read to the younger children in the school.

You could use the book to work on characterisation and settings. As it's written by children, they could also write extra chapters developing the characters. The children could also draw more Illustrations.

And the children could see if there is a different way of re-writing chapters or solving the problems of the journey in different ways.
They could also come up with a different ending for the story.

And they could certainly plot the sequel; what happened next? I would be very interested to hear their thoughts on that. But please bear in mind that the intellectual property rights (IPR) rests with the original creators!

If you would like to talk to me further about how I can help your creative writing programme in schools, please contact me on;

bellianita2@gmail.com
Or for more information about school's programmes from The Author in the Classroom:
https://thestorymoles.wordpress.com

For more information about the Author, Anita Belli
https://anitabellibooks2020.wordpress.com

Index of Children's names

This index is an indication of the pages where individual children are mentioned. It is not comprehensive; there were too many illustrations and text mentions to name them all, but I hope that this is a representative selection and you can find your child's input into this book.

The Great Fruitcake Pickleberry Theft

The Great Fruitcake Pickleberry Theft

Printed in Great Britain
by Amazon